A NOTE TO PARENTS

When your children are ready to "step into reading," giving them the right books—and lots of them—is as crucial as giving them the right food to eat. **Step into Reading Books** present exciting stories or information reinforced with lively, colorful illustrations that make learning to read fun, satisfying, and worthwhile. They are priced so that acquiring an entire library of them is affordable. And they are beginning readers with an important difference—they're written on three levels.

Step 1 Books, with their very large type and extremely simple vocabulary, have been created for the very youngest readers. **Step 2 Books** are both longer and slightly more difficult. **Step 3 Books,** written to mid-second-grade reading levels, are for the child who has acquired even greater reading skills.

To Lauren

Copyright © 1987 by Cathy East Dubowski and Mark Dubowski. All rights reserved under International
and Pan-American Copyright Conventions. Published in the United States by Random House, Inc.,
New York, and simultaneously in Canada by Random House of Canada Limited, Toronto.

Library of Congress Cataloging-in-Publication Data:
Dubowski, Cathy East. Pretty good magic. (Step into reading. A Step 2 book) SUMMARY: Presto's
attempt to impress the town of Forty Winks with a really spectacular trick produces more rabbits than
anyone expected. [1. Magicians—Fiction.   2. Rabbits—Fiction] I. Dubowski, Mark.   II. Title.   III.
Series: Step into reading. Step 2 book.   PZ7.D8544Pr   1987   [E]   87-4784
ISBN: 0-394-89068-X (trade); 0-394-99068-4 (lib. bdg.)

Manufactured in the United States of America   1 2 3 4 5 6 7 8 9 0

STEP INTO READING is a trademark of Random House, Inc.

Step into Reading

PRETTY GOOD MAGIC

By Cathy East Dubowski
and Mark Dubowski

A Step 2 Book

Random House 🏠 New York

The town of Forty Winks
was a nice, quiet place to live.
Folks got up every morning.
They went about their business.
And that was that.

If there was a fire,

they put it out.

If something broke,

they fixed it.

And if the newspaper came out late,
no one really cared.
There was never much news anyway.
Then one day Presto the Magician
came to town!

That night Presto put on a show.

Everyone was there.

Slowly the curtain opened.

Presto stepped out

into a bright circle of light.

"Get ready, folks,"

he said.

"The show is about to begin."

Then Presto did his tricks.

He was not a great magician.

He was not a bad magician.

Presto was a pretty good magician.

He turned three scarves into four.

He made a deck of cards fly.

Only two fell on the floor.

He even sawed a woman in half.

And after only three tries,

he put her back together!

"I have one more trick," Presto said.

"It is not my best trick.

It is not my worst trick.

But it is my favorite trick.

I always save it for last."

He tapped his tall black hat

with his magic wand.

Nothing happened.

Presto looked into the hat.
POOF! A cloud of smoke
blew up in his face.

"Now, that is more like it!" he said.
Presto put his hand into the hat ...

...and he pulled out
a rabbit!

The people clapped.

But they did not clap very loud

or very long.

"Thank you, Presto.

That was pretty good magic,"

said Mayor Huff.

Then everyone went home.

And that was that.

Presto walked back to his hotel.

He felt bad.

"Pretty good—that's me,"

Presto said sadly.

"Just once I want to do

some really great magic!"

Back at the hotel

Presto opened his book of magic.

He read page after page.

Then he found it!

The trick was called
"Rabbits by the Dozen."
Presto said to himself,
"If one rabbit is pretty good,
then dozens will be great!"
Presto held his magic wand
over his tall black hat.
He read from his book of magic:
   "Calling all rabbits
      and all of their cousins.
      Rabbit-ca-dabra!
      Dozens and dozens!"

Presto tapped the hat
with his magic wand
many, many times.

Nothing happened.

The hat just sat there.

Now Presto felt really bad.

"I am not even pretty good,"

he said. "I am awful!"

Presto turned out the light

and went to sleep.

Then something strange

began to happen.

The hat began to shake

and shake and shake.

A rabbit hopped out.

Then another and another.

Dozens and dozens of rabbits
hopped out of Presto's hat
all night long.

The next morning

Presto was snoring in bed.

Something tickled his nose.

Something tickled his toes.

He opened his eyes.

He could not believe what he saw!

23

There were rabbits on the bed...

rabbits on the floor...

rabbits in the dresser drawers.

Rabbits were everywhere!

Presto jumped out of bed.

"I did it!" he cried.

"I made dozens of rabbits appear!

The trick worked.

It just took a little time.

Tonight I will put on

another show.

Wait till the people

of Forty Winks see this!"

Then Presto raised his magic wand.

"Okay, rabbits," he said.

"Get back in the hat for now!"

Nothing happened.

The rabbits just sat there

and twitched their little pink noses.

"Oh, no!" said Presto.

He looked in his book of magic.

It told how to get

all the rabbits.

But it did not say how to

get rid of them!

Presto tried everything.

He said the magic words backward.

He made up his own magic words.

Nothing worked.

"I have to get these rabbits

out of here," he said.

It took three trips in
the elevator to get the
rabbits downstairs.

Presto's van was parked nearby.

He rushed the rabbits out of the hotel

and across the street.

SCREECH! BEEP! BEEP! SCREECH!

All the cars stopped and honked.

"Look at all those rabbits!"

everybody shouted.

Forty Winks had never had

a traffic jam before!

Presto sat down.

What a mess this was!

Everybody was laughing.

Mayor Huff stuck his head
out the window of his car.
He was not laughing.

"This is a nice, quiet town!" he yelled.
"It is my job to keep it that way!
These rabbits will have to go!
And so will you!"

Mayor Huff's dog was
in the car.
All the noise
made him nervous.
"Bow wow wow!"
barked the dog.
And away he went!

The rabbits saw the dog.

They got nervous too.

Away they went!

"Come back, dog!" shouted Mayor Huff.

"Come back, rabbits!" shouted Presto.

But the rabbits kept running.

Presto jumped into his van.

Now he had to catch

all those rabbits!

Presto found rabbits

in the coffee shop.

They took up all the seats!

He found rabbits in the bank.

"Stop!" shouted Presto.

"That is not lettuce. It's money!"

Presto found rabbits
in the shoe store.
"How cute!" a lady said.
"Little bunny slippers."
She tried to put them on,
but they ran away!

There were rabbits
in the department store.
They jumped up and down
on the beds.
Everybody laughed.
"See?" the sales clerk told the crowd.
"Our beds never lose their bounce!"

There were rabbits at the movies.
"Your ears are in the way!"
shouted the usher.
But nobody cared.
"These rabbits are funnier
than the movie!" someone said.

Presto even found rabbits
in school.
Children were laughing.
So was the teacher.
"We had so much fun
with your rabbits!"
she said.
Then Presto put the last rabbits
into his van.
He started
to drive away.

39

"Wait!" somebody shouted.

It was Mayor Huff.

All the people from town were with him.

"Presto, I was wrong,"

said the mayor.

"Your magic is not pretty good.

Your magic is great.

Forty Winks has never had

so much fun.

We want you to stay."

Presto said,

"I would love to stay.

But what will I do

with all these rabbits?"

Presto looked at all the people.

He looked at the school.

Then he had a great idea!

41

The very next day Presto opened
the Rabbit-ca-dabra School of Magic.

Everyone in town came
to learn Presto's tricks.

He taught them how
to turn three scarves into four.

He taught them how to make

a deck of cards fly!

45

He even taught them how to saw

a person in half—

and how to put him back together!

For the students' very last lesson,
Presto taught them his favorite trick.
He showed them how to pull a rabbit
out of a tall black hat.
When they learned that trick,
they got to keep the hat—
and the rabbit!

Now everyone in Forty Winks
has a rabbit of his own.
And every single rabbit has
its very own magician!